MAGIC CAMERA

MAGIC

CAMERA

MANUS PINKWATER

DODD, MEAD & COMPANY

N E W   Y O R K

FOR JILL

When Charles had the flu he read all his comic books. He read all his story books. He read all his school books. Some things he read twice. Then he read volume P of the *World Wide Children's Encyclopedia.* He only had volume P because someone had bought it at the supermarket for fifty-nine cents.

He read about pearls, the Pelew Islands, and the Peloponnesian War. He read about penguins, William Penn, and Pericles. He read about Persia, Peru, the Philippine Islands, and Phoenicia. He read about the phoenix, phonetics, and phosphorescence.

He read about photography. Charles liked that best. He read about lenses, and how light passes through a lens and turns upside-down, and makes an upside-down picture on the film. He read about cameras. He thought they were like magic boxes. He wished he could have one.

His family had a camera. They would take it along on trips, or take a picture of someone on their birthday. But it wasn't interesting like the cameras in the encyclopedia. It was just a box, and you looked through a little window, and pressed a button, and that was all. Charles wished he could have a camera that looked like magic, with cranks and knobs and buttons and switches.

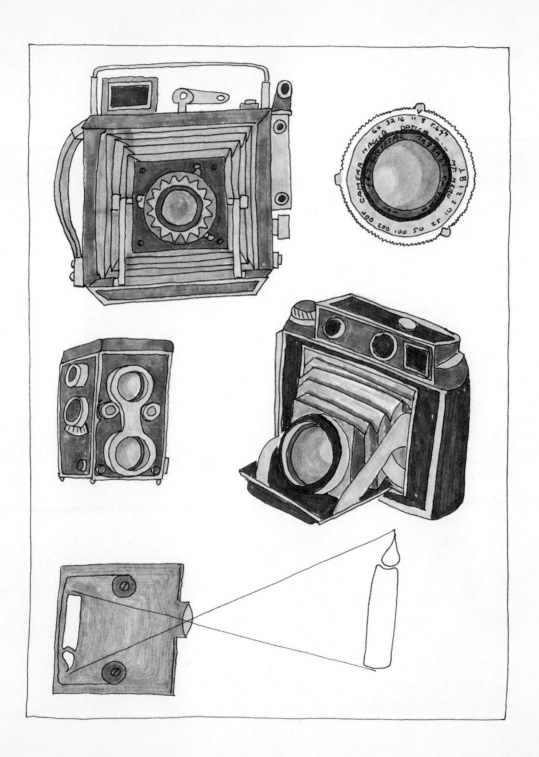

When Charles' father came home from work, he came into Charles' room to see how his boy was doing. Charles showed his father the pictures in the *World Wide Children's Encyclopedia.* He told him he wished he could have a camera. "We have a camera," his father said. "I don't see any reason why you can't use it whenever you want." Then Charles told his father about cameras that looked like magic, and he said he wanted a camera of his own.

"You know, old sport," his father said (Charles liked it when his father called him old sport; it usually meant he had a good idea), "I believe there is an old camera in a box in the cellar. I don't remember where it came from. Why don't I go down after supper and see if I can find it."

Charles had a hard time waiting until after supper. He hoped his father would be able to find the camera. He sat up in bed and waited. When his father came up from the cellar, he was all dusty and smiling.

Charles knew his father had found it. He was holding something behind his back. Then he showed Charles. It was a big leather box. Charles' father dangled it from a leather strap. The box was black and scuffed and scratched. It had a big brass lock on it. Charles' father pushed the lock with his thumb and clicked it open.

Then, out of the leather box, he took another box, also covered with leather, black bumpy leather, and there were shiny brass parts. Charles' father pressed a button. Click-click-click-clickety-snap! It jumped open like a jack-in-the-box. Little glass and metal things popped up and a beautiful deep red accordion thing came out. Little brass arms straightened their elbows and braced against angles of wood and brass and leather. The camera seemed to explode like a popcorn. It became twice the size of the box it had been. It was beautiful.

Charles looked at the camera. It looked at him. It had a deep blue lens that was like an eye. "This do for magic, sport?" his father asked.

Charles said it was just fine. His father put the camera on the table next to the bed, and left the room.

Having the flu made Charles sleepy. He took lots of little naps. He dozed off looking into the deep blue lens of the very magical, very beautiful camera.

Charles dreamed. He dreamed of taking pictures with the camera. He took a picture of a cat. He took a picture of a tree. He took a picture of the moon. He took a picture of telephone poles from the window of a speeding car. He took a picture of a rose garden.

When he woke up it was dark and quiet. Someone had switched off the light in his room. It was the middle of the night. Charles turned the light on. He wanted to see if the camera was really there, to see if he hadn't dreamed it too. It was there. The blue lens looked at him through his water glass. There were tiny bubbles in the water.

Charles reached over and touched a little button next to the lens. The camera clicked. The glass of water disappeared.

Charles came all the way awake. He felt funny. He noticed how quiet it was. He tried to think about the water glass disappearing like that, but he just couldn't manage it. It was too unlike anything he had ever thought about before. He couldn't get started thinking about it. So he sat in bed and looked at the camera. And the camera looked at him.

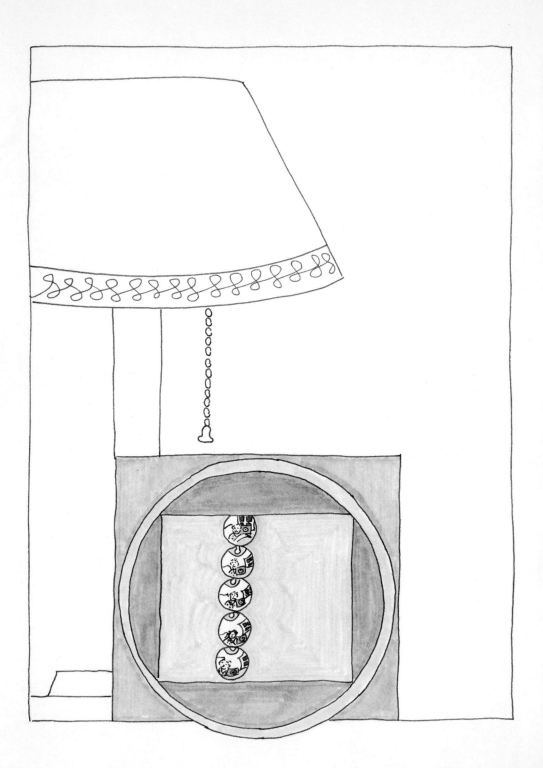

After a while Charles half-forgot about the water glass. It was too hard to think about anyhow. He thought he'd have a better look at the camera. He reached for it, and held it on his lap.

It was heavy. The leather covering felt nice, and the metal parts were smooth and shiny. He found a little window to look through to point the camera. When he looked through it, things were very sharp and clear. He looked through the window at the lamp on his bed table. He had never paid much attention to it before. Now he noticed all kinds of interesting things about it. For example, there was a little chain that turned the lamp on and off. The chain was made of tiny brass balls, each connected to the one above and below by a little pin. Each ball was like a mirror, and reflected the lamp, the room, Charles, and the camera. Charles looked at the chain through his camera for a long time.

Charles looked into the lens. There was a sort of spiral thing inside. He found a lever he could slide, and the spiral moved, and a little opening like the pupil in his eye got larger and smaller. A pointer moved, pointing to numbers engraved around the lens, "f 4.7, 5.6, 6.3, 8, 11, 16, 22, 32, 45." There were words written around the lens too, "Camera Magica Optica Cm 100 f 4.7." It was a nice camera.

There was a latch at the back of the camera. "This must be to put film in," he thought. Charles opened the latch, and the back of the camera swung open on hinges. Then Charles felt a rush of air, and thought he saw a flash of light. The whole room filled with the brightest moonlight he had ever seen.

The moonlight was bright. Of course it was, because the moon was inside Charles' bedroom! So were a tree, a rose garden, and a cat. Around the room, telephone poles whizzed, as though seen from the window of a moving car. All the things Charles had photographed in his dream were there, in his room. Charles looked at his night table to see if his water glass was there. It was. "This camera is more magic than I thought," he said.

The cat played in the rose garden, the moon shone, the tree spread its branches, and the telephone poles fairly flew along the walls. Charles sat on his bed. He wondered what his parents were going to say in the morning.

Then Charles had an idea. He opened the camera and looked inside. Nothing there. He closed the camera and looked through the little window. He pointed the camera at the moon. He clicked the button. The moon disappeared.

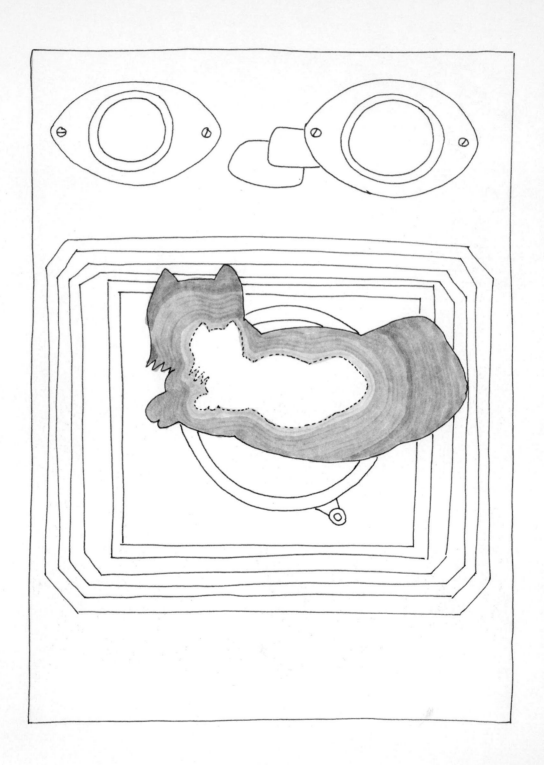

He pointed at the cat. Click. The cat was gone.

He pointed at the rose garden. Click. Gone. He pointed at the tree. Click. No tree. It took three clicks to get all the telephone poles.

Charles went to the window. He turned the back of the camera to the outside and opened the latch.

The moon rose up into the sky like a balloon. The tree and the rose garden planted themselves in the back yard. The cat perched on the windowsill and then bounded off into the night. The telephone poles whizzed out of the yard and up the street, around the corner and out of sight.

Charles felt better. His mother would be surprised to see the new tree and rose garden, but Charles wouldn't have to explain them.

He put his camera on the night table and went back to bed.

The next day his flu was much better. His father told him that the man in the camera store had said that Charles' camera was very old, and that they didn't make film for it any more.

"That's all right," Charles said. "I just like to look through it, anyhow."

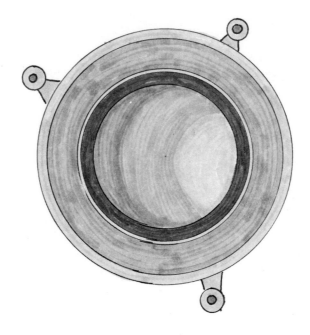